To my beloved sister, Soo Hyun,
who in her childhood is the real-life model for Bomi.
- S.H

어렸을적 모습을 떠올리며 그렸던 주인공 보미의 실제 모델인
내 사랑하는 동생 수현이에게.
- 언니가

Special thanks to my agent, Annabel Barker, and my publisher, Clair Hume,
for believing in my creative journey from the very start.

# THE COLOURS OF HOME

SALLY SOWEOL HAN

t&h

White mist hangs low
on the morning we leave.

The world below looks hazy through the clouds.

New country, new home.
Everything is different here ...

except for the silver moon.

We wind in and out of tunnels, through forests
of olive, jade and emerald. The same as …

… the park back home
where I once flew like a bird.

New birds are brilliantly blue.

Mum says, 'Seeing a Korean magpie means you will have a welcome guest.'

I think of the fairy wrens in our old backyard
and wonder when Grandma will visit.

Purple hydrangeas dance in the rain …

… swaying like the waltzing jacaranda trees near my old school.

We walk under grey birch trees
that stretch skyward.

I think of the ancient gum tree that stood
tall and wise at the end of our old street.

Dad takes me fishing in the turquoise bay where he grew up.

The water sparkles just like it did at
the beach where we learned to surf.

Orange is the sun setting over the rice field during harvest.
A time to share food with family and friends.

Orange is the earth where we camped last holidays.

Red is the strawberry pie we eat in winter ...

and the cherries I picked with Grandpa last summer.

The new year brings all the colours with it,
shimmering on the snow ...

… like they shimmered on the water.

And when I wake to a new day,
the same yellow sun is there to greet me.

First published in Australia in 2025 by Thames & Hudson Australia
Wurundjeri Country, 132A Gwynne Street, Cremorne, Victoria 3121



28 27 26 5 4 3



ISBN 978-1-76076-465-4

A catalogue record for this book is available from the National Library of Australia

Design by Claire Tice

Printed and bound in China by C&C Offset Printing Co., Ltd

MIX
Paper | Supporting responsible forestry
FSC® C008047

Thames & Hudson Australia wishes to acknowledge that Aboriginal and Torres Strait Islander peoples are the first storytellers of this nation and the Traditional Custodians of the land on which we live and work. We acknowledge their continuing culture and pay respect to Elders past and present.

thamesandhudson.com.au